She began to creep through the shadows on the lawn. The voice was clearer now, though it was still faint. And she thought that behind it she could hear other voices.

"Jessica! Jessica! Oh, if you can hear me, hurry! Please hurry."

Jessie moved faster, holding the cloak tightly around her. She knew now where the call was coming from.

It was coming from the secret garden.

Fairy Realm

BOOK 1

The Charm Bracelet

EMILY RODDA

ILLUSTRATIONS BY RAOUL VITALE

HARPERTROPHY®
AN IMPRINT OF HARPERCOLLINS PUBLISHERS

The Charm Bracelet
Copyright © 2000 by Emily Rodda
Illustrations copyright © 2003 by Raoul Vitale

www.harpercollinschildrens.com

Library of Congress Cataloging-in-Publication Data
Rodda, Emily.
    The charm bracelet / Emily Rodda. — 1st American ed.
        p.   cm. — (Fairy realm ; #1)
    Originally published: Sydney, N.S.W. : ABC Books, 2000.
    Summary: When Jessie searches for her ill grandmother's missing
charm bracelet, she is led to a magical world and finds she has a reason
and right to be there.
    ISBN 978-0-06-009585-7 (pbk.)
    [1. Grandmothers—Fiction. 2. Fairies—Fiction. 3. Bracelets—
Fiction. 4. Fantasy.] I. Title.
PZ7.R5996 Ch 2003   2002017276
[Fic]—dc21   CIP
                                                                 AC

Typography by Karin Paprocki
18 CG/BRR 10 9 8 7 6 5 4
❖
First Harper Trophy edition, 2009
Previously published by ABC Books for the
AUSTRALIAN BROADCASTING CORPORATION
GPO Box 9994 Sydney NSW 2001
Originally published under the name
Mary-Anne Dickinson as the Storytelling Charms Series 1994

CONTENTS

CHAPTER ONE

The secret garden

Jessie felt better once she was in the secret garden. She sat down right in the center of its smooth, small square of lawn and looked around.

Yes, here at least nothing at all had changed. This place still made her feel as safe and peaceful as it always had. Clustered around the edges of the lawn, her grandmother's favorite spiky gray rosemary bushes still filled the air with their sweet, tangy smell. Behind them the tall, clipped hedge still rose high on every side. When Jessie was little, she used to think the hedge made this part of her grandmother's garden very special. Its wall of leaves seemed to keep the whole world out.

But, thought Jessie, clasping her hands around her knees, it doesn't keep the world out. Not really. The secret garden's just a place at the bottom of Granny's real garden. It's a place where I can be alone for a while, and pretend things are still the way they were before Granny fell and sprained her wrist. Before Mum started worrying about Granny living alone, and decided she *must*, absolutely must, move out of Blue Moon, her big old house in the mountains, and come to live with us.

She remembered the last time she and her mother, Rosemary, had come to stay with Granny. It had been winter, nearly three months ago. There had been no talk of Granny moving then. Then, things had been very different.

Jessie had always loved winter at Blue Moon. Every evening, as it got dark, they would light a fire in the living room, and then Jessie and her mother would sit cuddled up on the big squashy chairs watching the flames while Granny made dinner.

"No, I don't want help. You sit down and rest,

Rosemary," Granny would say to Mum. "You work too hard. Let me look after you—just while you're here. I love to do it." And after a few minutes' protest, Mum would agree, and settle back gratefully, smiling.

Then for a while the only sounds they would hear would be the popping and snapping of the fire, the purring of Granny's big ginger cat, Flynn, crouched on a rug, and Granny's voice as she moved around the kitchen, singing the sweet songs that Jessie remembered from when she was a baby. There was one song that she had always especially loved. *Blue Moon floating, mermaids singing, elves and pixies, tiny horses* . . . it began. Jessie thought Granny had probably made it up, because it didn't rhyme, and the tune was lilting and strange.

Inside Blue Moon it was warm, cozy and safe. Outside, huge trees stretched bare branches to a cold black sky that blazed with stars, and in the morning a dusting of white frost crackled under your feet when you walked on the grass.

It had always seemed strange and magical to

Jessie. At home there were no big trees and no frost. And the city lights seemed to drown the brightness of the stars.

But if winter in the mountains was magical, spring was even better. In spring everything sparkled. The bare trees began to bud with new leaves of palest green, and in their shade bluebells and snowdrops clustered. Bees buzzed around the lilac bushes that bent their sweet, heavy heads beside the house. Butterflies of every color and size danced among the apple blossom. In spring it was as if Blue Moon was waking up after a long sleep. Everywhere there were new beginnings.

But not this spring, Jessie thought sadly. This spring was more like an ending. She'd been feeling sad ever since her mother had told her about the plan to take Granny home with them at the end of this visit.

"Don't you want Granny to live with us, Jessie?" her mother had finally asked her, as they drove up the winding road that led from the city to the mountains. "You two have always been so close, especially since your dad died. I thought you'd love the idea."

Jessie tried to explain. "It's just that . . . I can't really imagine Granny away from Blue Moon," she said. She turned her head away, pretending to look out the window, but really not wanting her mother to see the tears she could feel prickling in her eyes. "And . . . I'll miss . . . coming up here," she burst out. "I'll miss the house, and the trees, and the secret garden."

"Oh, darling, of course you will!" Mum took one hand off the steering wheel to stroke Jessie's long red hair. "So will I. Blue Moon's my old home, remember. I love it, just like you do. But Jessie, it's been five years since Grandpa died. And you know how worried I've been about Granny living all alone without anyone to look after her." She smiled. "My dad might have been the artist in the family, but he was a very practical man all the same. You wouldn't remember, I suppose. But he was sensible, and took no risks. Which is more than you can say for Granny, bless her heart."

Jessie in fact did remember Grandpa quite well, even though she'd been so young when he

5

died. His name was Robert Belairs. His paintings had been sold all over the world and were in many books. But to Jessie he was just Grandpa, a tall, gentle man with kind blue-gray eyes, a short white beard and a beautiful smile. She remembered how he always let her watch him paint in his upstairs studio at Blue Moon. And she remembered the paintings he worked on there—the soft, misty mountain landscapes, and the fairyland scenes for which he'd become so famous.

It was the fairy pictures that Jessie had especially loved. Sitting quietly on a stool beside him, she used to watch with wonder as a fantasy world came to life under her grandfather's brush, a mysterious and beautiful world full of golden light. Lots of these paintings hung on the walls of Blue Moon, because every year, on Granny's birthday, Grandpa had painted a special picture just for her. He'd finished the last one just before he died.

Robert Belairs' fairyland was a world of pretty cottages, treehouses and shining castles, and elfin-faced people in wonderful floating clothes. He always called these people "the Folk." The most beautiful and royal-looking of the women had long golden-red hair and green eyes like Jessie's own. This had pleased her very much, though she knew that Grandpa wasn't really painting her. He'd always painted his fairy princesses that way. People used to laugh and say that was why he'd fallen in love with her grandmother in the first place. Granny's hair was white now, of course, but when she had first come to Blue Moon to marry Robert Belairs her hair had been as red as Jessie's.

Grandpa's paintings were also full of busy gnomes, dwarfs, pixies and elves, thin little brownies, and tiny flower and rainbow fairies with gossamer wings. There were sometimes miniature horses, too, their manes threaded with ribbons and tiny bells. Jessie had really loved those. She had thought her grandfather was very clever to be able to paint such pictures. Maybe he was a bit magical himself.

And yes, she remembered how carefully he had looked after Granny, too. When Mum and Jessie had visited Blue Moon in those days, it was Granny who cooked the delicious food they ate, who talked and laughed, who suggested all sorts of outings and adventures and never expected anything to go wrong. But it was Grandpa who packed the extra box of matches for the picnic, "just in case." It was Grandpa who took the umbrella when they went on a walk, "just in case." It was Grandpa who made sure there were spare keys to all the doors, "just in case."

Granny used to tease him about it. She'd reach up to pat his cheek, the gold charm bracelet she always wore jingling on her wrist. "You always expect the worst, Robert. Don't worry so. All will be well," she'd say. And he'd smile, and touch her hand. "Better to be safe than sorry, princess," he'd answer. And quite often he was right.

Jessie could understand why Mum thought Granny couldn't exist safely without him. But she just knew Mum was wrong. Her mind went back to the argument they'd had in the car on the way up to Blue Moon.

"Granny tripped over that stray kitten that came in!" she'd protested. "That had nothing to do with being alone, Mum. That could happen to anyone, any time. And she only sprained her wrist."

"But Jessie, it could have been so much worse!" Her mother had frowned. "If she'd hurt her leg or something she could have lain there in pain for days without being able to call for help." Her hands had tightened on the steering wheel. "You have to be sensible about this, Jessie," she'd said firmly. "And so does Granny. Both of you have to listen to me for a change. What's needed round here is a bit of common sense!"

Now, sitting in the secret garden, Jessie realized that her mother was really very like Grandpa. She had his kind blue-gray eyes and his strong practical streak. She wasn't like Granny at all. But Jessie was. She knew that quite well. For one thing, she looked like Granny. She was going to be taller, of course: that was obvious, since already they were about the same height. Jessie wore an old gray cloak of Granny's for a dressing gown when she came to stay at Blue Moon, and even when she was in bare feet it didn't trail on the ground.

It was from Granny that Jessie had inherited her red hair, green eyes and pointed chin. She had been named Jessica after Granny, too. But, more important than name or looks, Jessie and her grandmother shared a love of stories, songs and fantasy that made them really enjoy each other's company.

And there was something else. They simply understood each other. Jessie always knew how Granny was feeling about things, and Granny always knew how Jessie was feeling, too. It had been like that ever since Jessie could remember.

Was that why, when Jessie had run into Granny's bedroom after they'd arrived at Blue Moon an hour ago, she had immediately felt so worried and sad? Was that why she hadn't been able to bear staying there, but had had to escape to the secret garden? Was that why . . . ?

Jessie sat perfectly still. Without warning, a thought had whirled into her mind. She began to shiver, her eyes wide and startled, her hands gripping the soft grass. Suddenly she had become terribly sure of something. Granny was in trouble. Real trouble. It wasn't just a matter of a sprained wrist, or sadness, or loneliness. It was something far more dangerous.

She sprang to her feet. She didn't know where the thought had come from. But now it was there, she knew it was true. And she had to do something about it. She didn't know what. But she had to help. She had to!

She began running for the house.

CHAPTER TWO

The Missing Bracelet

At her grandmother's bedroom door Jessie hesitated. Her heart was thumping. She smoothed her tangled hair and tried to calm down. Mum and Nurse Allie would still be with Granny. They'd be alarmed if she burst into the room in a panic.

She felt the soft tap of a paw on her ankle, gasped with fright, and looked down to meet the solemn golden eyes of Flynn, her grandmother's cat. He had been sitting so quietly in the dim hallway that she hadn't noticed him. She crouched to stroke his soft fur.

13

"Are you keeping guard on Granny's door, Flynn?" she asked him. "Won't Nurse Allie let you inside?"

He stared at her, unblinking.

"She would, you know, if only you wouldn't fight with the gray kitten," Jessie whispered, moving her hand around to scratch him under the chin. "It wasn't the kitten's fault that Granny fell, you know, Flynn. It was an accident."

Flynn rumbled in his throat, a noise more like a growl than a purr.

"Don't worry," Jessie soothed him. "Granny will be feeling better soon. Nurse Allie's going home now that we're here. Mum's a nurse, too, and Granny will be quite all right with her. So tonight I'll let you into Granny's room. The kitten can stay out, for a change. Everything's going to be all right, Flynn."

But when she opened the door and slipped into the bedroom, she wasn't so sure. When they'd first arrived, Granny had been sitting in her comfortable chair by the window. Now she was lying in bed, looking pale and ill. Rosemary was sitting beside her, hands clasped on the flowery bedcover, while in the corner of the room Nurse Allie, plump and busy, measured out medicine. The little gray kitten, Flynn's enemy, purred softly on the window seat.

Granny's long white hair, braided into a thick plait, trailed over the pillows. One wrist was heavily bandaged. The bandage was much more obvious now that she was lying down and her arm was out of the sling she'd been wearing earlier.

She smiled faintly at Jessie. "Where have you been, Jessie?" she asked. Even her voice sounded different. It seemed to have lost its music.

"I've been to the secret garden," Jessie said, moving over to stand beside the bed.

Granny smiled again. "Oh, yes," she murmured. "The secret garden. You love it, don't you, Jessie?"

"Maybe you could come there with me, tomorrow morning," Jessie suggested eagerly, taking her hand.

"Well, that might be a little difficult for Granny, dear," beamed Nurse Allie, bringing the medicine over to the bed. "But you could sit out on the front verandah for a while, Mrs. Belairs, couldn't you? The fresh air would do you the world of good. Cheer you up!"

"We'll see," said Granny softly. "I just feel . . . so tired." Her eyelids fluttered closed.

Jessie looked despairingly around the room. Why was Granny like this? She saw that Nurse Allie was shaking her head at Mum in disappointment. Cheerful Nurse Allie, with her crisp curls and smart uniform, had tried very hard to make things pleasant for Granny while she waited for Mum and Jessie to come.

She'd used every trick she knew to brighten up the bedroom. She'd brought in vases of spring flowers. She'd opened the curtains to let in the sunshine. She'd let the gray kitten play on the rug. She'd noticed that the dark, mysterious painting on the wall facing the bed, the last painting Grandpa had done before he died, made Granny cry, so she'd taken it away and put a pretty mountain scene in its place.

But nothing had worked. Granny lay quiet and

listless in her bed, or sat obediently in her chair, without showing any sign of cheering up or getting well.

Jessie was still for a moment. Then she noticed something. She stared. Why hadn't she noticed this before?

"Granny, where's your bracelet?" she asked. Never before had she seen Granny without her gold bracelet, so thickly hung with charms that it tinkled on her wrist with every movement.

The old woman's eyelids slowly opened. "Bracelet?" she mumbled. She looked confused, and then there was a flash of memory and panic in her eyes. Her fingers tightened on Jessie's hand. "It's lost!" she muttered. "Jessie . . . it's gone. They . . . must have taken it off while they were fixing my wrist." She struggled to rise from her pillow. "Jessie, you must find it for me. You must! I need it!"

"Now, now, don't let's get ourselves into a froth!" crooned Nurse Allie, frowning at Jessie. She pressed Granny gently back on to the pillows. "Now, we've been through all this, dear. We know the bracelet must be somewhere, don't we? It's quite safe. It's been put away in some drawer or other, that's all."

"I must have it!" protested Granny, moving her head restlessly.

"You just concentrate on getting better, Mum," said Rosemary. "We'll worry about the bracelet later."

"But time is running out! It's nearly my seventieth birthday!" Granny cried. Then she stopped, and a strange, puzzled expression crossed her face. "My birthday? Why does that matter?" she whispered.

Nurse Allie stepped forward briskly. "A little rest is what you need, I think, dear," she said, shooting a warning look at Rosemary and Jessie. "All this excitement! Goodness me!"

"Sorry, Nurse," said Rosemary. She stood up and pushed Jessie a little crossly to the door. Jessie could see there was no point in arguing. Both Mum and Nurse Allie thought she was making Granny upset. She let herself be ushered from the room.

Flynn looked at Jessie and her mother with

wide eyes as they closed the door softly behind them, but he made no move to follow them out to the back of the house. He just settled back to his guard duty, still as a statue, in the dim hallway.

"Jessie, you mustn't worry Granny," Rosemary said sternly as they reached the kitchen. "Not about the charm bracelet, or the secret garden, or anything. She's not well. She has to have peace and quiet." She began pulling things out of cupboards, getting ready to start dinner. Then she turned around and tried to smile.

"Look, darling, don't worry too much," she said. "It's only natural for Granny to be depressed. Just think about it. Her wrist must be very sore. And it's her birthday the day after tomorrow. It wasn't long after her birthday five years ago that Grandpa died. It makes her sad to think about it."

"But Mum . . ." Jessie looked at her mother's kind, worried face and thought better of what she'd been about to say. Mum wouldn't understand about the feeling of danger she'd had in the secret garden. And she wouldn't understand why she felt the charm bracelet was so important. After all, Jessie didn't really understand it herself!

All Jessie knew was that Granny was in trouble. And that the charm bracelet she always wore was missing. And that for some reason the bracelet had to be found before Granny's birthday the day after tomorrow. Jessie clenched her fists. She made herself a promise that she would find the bracelet if she had to look behind every cushion and in every drawer in the house to do it! After dinner she'd check Granny's room. Then she'd do the living room and the kitchen. She'd be sure to find it before bedtime.

But bedtime came and still the bracelet had not been found.

Jessie lay cuddled up in bed in the small room that was always hers at Blue Moon and thought hard. Of course there were many more places she could look. But she couldn't see how the bracelet could have got into one of the spare rooms, for example, or the dining room, or the sunroom either.

She closed her eyes. The bed was warm and

soft, and the sheets smelled faintly of rosemary. She was very tired. Her thoughts began to drift. In the morning she'd try again. In the morning . . .

Her eyes flew open again. She could have sworn she'd heard a very faint tinkling sound. It sounded just like the charm bracelet when it jingled on Granny's wrist. And it had come from outside, in the garden. She was sure of it.

She threw back the covers, jumped out of bed and ran to the window. Outside, grass and flowers shone in the moonlight. The trees held their budding branches up to the sky, throwing deep shadows on the lawn. Jessie strained her eyes, but there was nothing more to be seen. Nothing but the gray kitten, slinking through the trees toward the secret garden.

Jessie shivered. She left the window and ran back to bed, jumping in and pulling the covers tightly around her. There was no one out there. She must have imagined the sound. She closed her eyes again and tried not to think about the bracelet. Again the warmth of the bed stole around her. Then, suddenly, she thought of a place she hadn't looked. When Nurse Allie had taken Grandpa's painting off Granny's bedroom wall, she'd put it in his studio for safekeeping. Jessie heard her tell Mum so. Maybe she'd absent-mindedly put the bracelet there, too.

The more Jessie thought about it, the more likely it seemed. The studio. First thing in the morning, she'd look there. With a sigh of relief she turned on her side, and in a few moments was asleep.

CHAPTER THREE

The Call

The next morning, before breakfast, Jessie went to Grandpa's studio. She turned the key in the door and let herself in. It was a big, beautiful room painted white. The early morning light streamed through its tall windows.

Jessie sighed. The room reminded her so much of Grandpa. It still smelled of paint, canvas and paper. The stool she had always sat on while she was watching him paint stood in one corner. His paints and brushes, sketchpads and other things lay on the bench as though he was about to come and use them any minute.

She noticed that the picture Nurse Allie had taken from Granny's room was leaning against a table near the door. She looked at it curiously. It certainly wasn't as pretty as most of the others Grandpa had done, she decided. It was dim and very mysterious looking, and there were no people, animals or fairies in it. It showed an archway in a wild-looking dark green hedge covered with splodges of gray. Through the archway you could dimly see what lay beyond—a pebbly road, a few shadowy bushes and a gray sky in which a pale blue moon floated. A blue moon, thought Jessie. Grandpa must have been thinking about this house when he painted that.

Carefully she tipped the painting forward so she could look at the back. She knew Grandpa often put the names of his paintings there. But this time there was no name. Only a white card, painted with a sprig of rosemary, and some words in Grandpa's firm, looping handwriting: *For my princess on her birthday. Better to be safe than sorry. All my love, always, Robert.* Then there was a date. Almost exactly five years ago.

Holding her breath, Jessie gently let the painting tip back into place again. No wonder it made Granny cry. It mightn't be the prettiest picture Grandpa had painted, but it was his last present to her, and the message showed how much he'd loved her.

Biting her lip, Jessie looked around at the benches and shelves that lined the studio. Everything was neat and clean. Everything was in its place. There was no sign at all of the charm bracelet.

She left the studio and hurried to Granny's room. She found her sitting in her chair by the window, her arm in a white sling. Flynn, purring like rumbling thunder, was lying beside her. The gray kitten was nowhere to be seen. Granny looked up and smiled as Jessie came in and gave her a kiss.

"Your mother was wondering where you were, Jessie," she said. "I think she wants you to have breakfast."

"I've been looking for your bracelet, Granny," said Jessie eagerly. "I haven't found it yet, but I just came to tell you that you mustn't worry. I won't give up. I'm going to look everywhere till it's found."

Her grandmother's smile slowly faded and a puzzled line deepened between her eyebrows. "Bracelet?" she asked softly. "What bracelet is that, Jessie?"

Shocked, Jessie stared at her. "Your charm bracelet!" she burst out. "You know. The bracelet you always wear. The one that got lost."

"Oh . . ." Granny looked confused and uncertain. She raised her unbandaged hand to her forehead. Her fingers trembled slightly. "Oh . . . I'm sorry, dear. I'm . . . getting a bit forgetful, I think. I'm not quite sure . . ."

Flynn growled in his throat.

"Breakfast, Mum!" announced Rosemary's cheery voice. She came in bearing a tray of fruit, toast and tea, and put it down on a side table. "Oh, here you are, Jessie!" she exclaimed. "I didn't know where you'd got to."

Jessie looked from Granny to her mother and back again. Her throat felt tight. Only yesterday

Granny had been worrying herself sick about the charm bracelet. How could she have forgotten it so soon? She mumbled something, backed out the door and ran for the kitchen.

Jessie searched for the charm bracelet all day, but when night fell she still hadn't found it. And she was the only one who cared. Granny now seemed truly to have forgotten that the bracelet had ever existed. And Mum, busy packing and organizing things for the move back to town, was too distracted to think much about it.

"Don't worry yourself too much, Jessie," she said kindly that evening, as she watched Jessie going through the drawers in the living room yet again. "The bracelet's slipped down behind something, probably. Or got mixed up with some other stuff in Granny's room. It'll turn up in the end."

Maybe, thought Jessie. But not soon enough. Tomorrow's Granny's birthday. We're running out of time. She paused, confused by her own thoughts. Running out of time? For what? She closed the drawer in which she'd been searching, and rubbed her forehead with a tired hand. Mum had said not to worry but Jessie couldn't help it. And something else was worrying her far more than the missing bracelet.

She glanced at her mother. She couldn't keep it to herself any longer.

"Granny doesn't remember her bracelet any more!" she whispered. "When I talk to her about it she doesn't know what I mean!" She bent her head, tears in her eyes.

Rosemary's face softened. "Oh, Jessie, darling, don't be sad." She put her arm around Jessie's waist. "You know that sometimes when people get older they can be forgetful. And Granny hasn't been well. She had a bad shock when she fell. It's quite natural that she's a bit confused now. It's not something to be scared of or anything."

Jessie nodded and sniffed. "I know that," she said. "But Granny's not very old. She's only sixty-nine. Simone at school's great-grandmother is a hundred and one, and *she* remembers things. And anyway, Mum, whatever else Granny forgot, how could she forget the charm bracelet? She used to tell me every charm on it was a memory of something special. Every charm had a story. The heart, and the fish, and the apple, and the key, and . . ."

Her mother patted her shoulder. "I know," she soothed. "I know. It's hard for you to understand. But Granny's been living alone here for too long, Jessie. She's been living in the past. She'll be so much better when she's away from here. Believe me."

Jessie wasn't so sure. When she crawled into bed that night, her thoughts were racing around in her head so much that she was afraid she would lie awake all night. But she was very tired and it wasn't long before she was lulled to sleep in the warm, cozy bed.

She slept very deeply. The moon climbed higher in the sky and shone through the window, but Jessie slept on. There were sounds in the night but she didn't hear them. The hours slipped by. And then . . .

Thud! A heavy weight landed on Jessie's feet. She opened her eyes, blinking in the darkness.

31

Her heart pounded. What was happening? She felt something moving on the bedclothes. And then she was staring into the golden gaze of Flynn, and his soft paw was patting her cheek.

She wet her dry lips and sat up. "What is it?" she whispered. Flynn stared at her, then looked toward the window.

Jessie rubbed her eyes. Was this a dream? No, Flynn was really there, and again he was looking at the window. He jumped from the bed and walked over to it, his tail high. He looked back at her. He wanted her to come with him.

Jessie got out of bed and went to the window just as she had the night before. She looked out. But again there was nothing to be seen. Not even the gray kitten, slinking among the trees. There was nothing . . .

And then she heard it. The faintest possible sound. A voice. She strained her ears to hear.

"Jessica! Jessica!"

Jessie's mouth fell open in shock. Someone was calling her name! She looked wildly at Flynn. He padded to the bedroom door, looking back at her over his shoulder.

"Flynn, what is it?" hissed Jessie. He went out the door and then came back in again. His golden eyes were fixed on hers. It was obvious that he wanted her to follow.

"Jessica!" The voice was a little clearer now. It sounded urgent, and tired, as though it had been calling for a long time.

Jessie ran to the corner cupboard and pulled out Granny's old gray cloak. It would be chilly in the garden. She threw the cloak around her shoulders and followed Flynn.

He padded to the back door and then stood back while she opened it and slipped outside into the cool night air.

"Aren't you coming with me?" she whispered, looking back at him. But somehow she knew the answer even before he sat down on the doorstep, head up, paws pressed together. He had to wait here. He had to guard Granny. That was his job. Jessie had to go into the night and answer the strange call alone.

She began to creep through the shadows on the

lawn. The voice was clearer now, though it was still faint. And she thought that behind it she could hear other voices.

"Jessica! Jessica! Oh, if you can hear me, hurry! Please hurry."

Jessie moved faster, holding the cloak tightly around her. She knew now where the call was coming from.

It was coming from the secret garden.

"where am i?"

H olding her breath, Jessie pushed open the
door in the hedge and stepped inside.

There was no one there. The scent of rosemary
wafted about her as she stood motionless on the
smooth grass. She took another step . . .

Suddenly there was a sighing, whispering
sound, a rush of air against her face, and a swirl
of mist clouding her eyes. Jessie's cloak snapped
away from her fingers. Her hair blew, crackling,
around her head. She gasped with fear.

And then she was no longer in the secret
garden. She was no longer anywhere at all she

knew. And the voice was calling out in glee: "We've got her! I told you so! I told you . . ." and then it broke off and cried out in surprise and horror. "Oh, no! Oh no-o-o!"

Jessie gazed around her. She felt rather than saw that her cloak had slipped to the ground. Her hair was tangled on her shoulders. Far away she could hear singing.

She was standing on a pebbly road that ran beside a thick, dark hedge—a hedge much, much higher and stronger than the hedge of the secret garden, but marked all over with great gray patches of dead and dying wood. The air was sweet and shadowy. A memory stirred in her. Abruptly she looked up. There, sure enough, was a soft gray sky and, floating in it, a blue moon. But when she looked back at the hedge she could see no archway. There was no way she could tell how she had come through the hedge at all.

"This is a disaster!" snapped an angry voice.

Jessie spun around. Behind her, gaping at her in astonishment, were a fat little woman with eyes like black beads, her head wound up in a scarf; a thin, depressed-looking elf with long pointed ears that drooped at the tips; and a perfect miniature white horse with ribbons in its mane and a very cross expression on its face. Jessie was astounded to realize that it was the horse who had spoken.

"A disaster!" it growled again. "How could this have happened?" It rounded on the fat little woman. "Patrice! I thought you said . . ."

"This is definitely the Door," the woman called Patrice fluttered. "Maybelle, I promise you, it is *definitely*—"

"We're doomed!" wailed the elf. "Doomed! Now we've used up all the magic. And the Door's shut again! And we still haven't found her. We got some human child instead. Oh, doom! Doom! Oh I *knew* this would never work. I knew it!"

Jessie covered her mouth with both hands to stop herself from screaming. Where was she? Who were these people?

There was a shout and a stomping sound in the distance.

"Look out!" hissed Maybelle, shaking her mane. "The Royal Guard!"

"Oh, no!" squeaked the elf. He flapped his hands and began to run helplessly this way and that. "Oh, what next? Now we're for it! Now we're for it!"

"Hide her, Patrice! Quick! Over there!" ordered Maybelle, ignoring him.

Patrice put her arm around Jessie and hustled her away behind some nearby bushes. The noise of marching feet grew louder. With a last despairing squeak the elf leaped into the air and hung there, with his hands over his eyes.

Maybelle rolled her own eyes in disgust, then lowered her nose and began calmly to eat grass as if nothing at all unusual was happening.

"Stay still as still, dearie," breathed Patrice in Jessie's ear.

Jessie had no intention of moving. She had never been so scared in her life. She huddled close to the ground, hardly daring to breathe.

In a few moments a group of soldiers in smart uniforms marched out of the dimness. Their booted feet scrunched on the pebbles of the roadway. Patrice squeezed Jessie's hand in her own small one. Jessie trembled and she closed her eyes. Her cloak was still lying where it had fallen on the road. The soldiers were certain to see it there as they walked past. Then they would know a stranger was here. And they would start to search. And then . . .

"Halt!" The leading guard barked the order, and with a stamp the whole troop stopped dead, right in front of the spot where Jessie and Patrice were hiding.

"Five minutes' rest," said the leading guard. The word was passed along the line, and one by one the guards thankfully broke away from the line and sat down on the grass. The leader glanced at the shivering elf in the air and snorted with tired amusement. She stretched her back and looked at the moon. "It's midnight, Loris," she said to the man next to her. "The big day's come at last."

"They're cutting it a bit fine if you ask me," he answered gruffly. He flicked a finger at a bare patch in the dark, looming hedge. "This won't last much longer. They say sunrise marks the fifty years exactly. The Lady came back last night, didn't she? Why hasn't she fixed up the magic by now? Why wait till the last minute?"

The leader shrugged. "I suppose she knows what she's doing," she replied. "But I tell you what, I'll be glad to see the hedge back to normal again, Loris. It's dying fast. And without it we'll never keep the Others out. Too many of them."

The man grunted his agreement. "They say there are thousands of them, just waiting. They know the story. They've been hoping that the Lady won't come back. They've been hoping that the magic'll all run out, and the hedge'll die." He jerked his head to where Maybelle was innocently grazing nearby. "And you know what they'll do then," he added grimly.

Maybelle raised her head and shook her white mane.

Behind the bushes, Jessie felt Patrice's hand tighten on her own.

"Sshh!" warned the leader. "No point in getting creatures all upset. And anyhow, there's nothing to worry about, Loris. The Lady did come back, didn't she? Just like she said she would. And today's the day. Listen to those mermaids singing. They've gathered in the Bay. Hundreds of them. They know it's time. By morning the hedge'll be its old self again."

"Lucky this magic business only happens once in a blue moon," growled Loris. "I don't like it."

"Can't say I care for it much either," grinned the leader. She pulled her cap straighter on her head. "All right, Loris. They've had enough of a rest. Let's get going."

Loris turned and shouted. Grumbling, the rest of the guards got up and formed into a line again.

"Forward!" barked the leader. And off the troop marched. Left, right, left, right, along the pebbled road. In a few moments everything was quiet again.

Carefully Patrice and Jessie clambered to their feet and crept out into the open. Jessie ran and picked up her cloak, which was still lying beside the hedge. It was a wonder that the guards hadn't noticed it, she thought. She hugged it to her for a moment. It was soft and warm, and smelled of home.

Maybelle trotted over to them. She glanced disdainfully up at the elf, who was still floating in the air, his hands firmly over his eyes.

"They've gone, Giff!" she called. "Come down!"

But the elf didn't move.

"Giff!" the horse fumed. She turned to Patrice and pawed the ground. "That fool of an elf," she said through gritted teeth, "is going to be the death of me."

"He's probably blocked his ears as well as his eyes, poor thing," said Patrice comfortably. "He can't hear you." She dug in her pocket and pulled out some round white sweets that smelled strongly of peppermint. "Giff!" she shouted. Then, with expert aim, she sent a mint hurtling through the air, hitting the floating elf neatly on the back of the neck.

With a cry of fright Giff threw out his arms and legs, and fell to the ground with a thump. He lay on the grass, his ears quivering with fright. "What hit me?" he quavered.

"Must have been a mosquito, dearie," said Patrice mildly. "Look, the guards have gone. Now we've got to go, too. It's not safe out here. We have to decide what we're going to do."

Giff's ears drooped even more. He beat his fists on the grass. "What's the point?" he wailed. "The plan's in ruins. We failed. Completely, absolutely, utterly. We're doomed!"

"Well, if we're doomed," snorted Maybelle, "let's at least be doomed inside. Come on!"

Giff stumbled to his feet, sniffing, but Jessie stood her ground. She'd had enough of this. "I'm not going anywhere until you tell me what's going on!" she said firmly. She turned to Maybelle. A horse she might be, but she definitely seemed to be the leader in this group.

"You tell me!" she demanded. "Where am I? What is this place? And what's happening to the hedge that you need magic to fix? And who are the Others? How did I get here?" She took a deep breath. "And the main thing is, how do I get back?"

CHAPTER FIVE

The Magic

Maybelle's eyelids fluttered. She tossed her mane uncomfortably. "Ah . . . we'll go into all that later," she said.

Jessie stamped her foot. "No, we won't!" she insisted. "We'll go into it now!"

Patrice gave a little cough. "I really think we should tell the child everything, Maybelle," she said. "We owe her that much, don't you think?"

Maybelle humphed and tossed her mane again. "All right," she said finally. "All right. But I insist that we go inside. The guards might be back this way, and we simply can't afford to be

47

caught here with her."

"The palace is just along the road a bit," put in Patrice, tucking her arm through Jessie's. "And a cup of hot chocolate wouldn't go astray, would it? We can talk on the way."

Hot chocolate in a palace? Jessie looked at her in wonder. But Giff was licking his lips and Maybelle had already started trotting along the road, so she shrugged her shoulders and let Patrice lead her away.

"It's like this," Patrice began, as they hurried along to catch up with Maybelle. "This hedge, you see, is the border of the Realm. It keeps us safe from the Others."

"Who—" began Jessie. Giff interrupted.

"Trolls!" he panted, his eyes wide with fright. "Trolls and—ogres and—goblins—and dragons— and—giants—and—monsters—and—and—"

"And all sorts of nasties, dearie," Patrice said, nodding. She sighed. "They live in the Outlands, on the other side of the hedge."

"But I thought *we* lived there," said Jessie in surprise.

Patrice shook her head. "Oh no, dearie," she said. "Yours is a quite different world. The Doors to your world open by magic. But the Outlands is part of *this* world. And the Outlands creatures would love to get into the Realm, my word they would. But they can't, you see? The hedge keeps them out."

Ahead of them, Maybelle had slowed to a walk. As Jessie watched, she darted into a grove of tall, pale-leaved trees by the side of the road.

"Come on!" urged Patrice.

They followed Maybelle, and soon Jessie saw that behind the trees rose the turrets and spires of a great golden palace, just like the one in her grandfather's paintings. Light streamed from a vast doorway directly below a row of tall windows that stretched across the front of the palace. Jessie was filled with excitement. She imagined walking in that door like a princess and wished she was wearing proper clothes. A nightdress and bare feet didn't seem right for her first visit to a palace. She wondered if she should put on her cloak.

But to her disappointment the others ignored

the main entrance. Instead, they slipped around the side of the building and led her to a very small door hidden behind some bushes.

"In here," whispered Patrice, producing a key.

A few moments later they were in a narrow hallway, and then a small, snug kitchen. Jessie looked around in surprise. "Is this where they cook the food for the whole palace?" she asked.

Patrice burst out laughing, her little black eyes twinkling. "Oh, hardly, dearie!" she giggled. "The palace kitchens are a hundred times bigger than this. This is just for cooking my own meals in my time off. I'm the palace housekeeper, you know. Used to be nurse to all the palace babies when I was younger. Now, you sit down and I'll make you that hot chocolate." She tied a white apron around her plump waist and began bustling around, getting chocolate and milk and cream, and putting cookies on a plate.

Everything seemed so ordinary that for a moment Jessie quite forgot that she was in a very strange place, with some very strange people, and that she had a lot of questions still to be answered.

Then she caught sight of Maybelle leaning comfortably against the table with her back legs crossed, and remembered. "Why do the ogres and trolls and things even *want* to get into your world?" she asked.

Maybelle gave a bitter snort. "They're a nasty lot through and through, and they just want to destroy every beautiful thing they see," she said. "But apart from that, they want the gold that lies in our riverbeds. They're gold mad!" She sniffed. "And of course," she added casually, "they want me."

"You?" Jessie stared.

"Me, and all my friends and relations," Maybelle said. "They want to use us as slaves to work in their mines. In the dark, underground. Harnessed to carts full of rocks. Huh!" She lifted her head and stared straight ahead. Her words might sound disdainful, but Jessie could see that underneath she was afraid. She felt Patrice gripping her arm. The little woman was afraid, too.

"They won't get in, Maybelle," quavered Giff. "Will they?"

"If the hedge keeps going the way it is, I don't see how we can keep them out," huffed the little horse.

"And that, dearie, is where you come in," sighed Patrice, darting a look at Jessie as she put cups filled to the brim with foaming chocolate drink on the table. "Or where you *would* have come in, if you were who we thought you were."

"I don't understand!" cried Jessie.

"I'm not surprised," snapped Maybelle. She heaved herself away from the table and glared at Patrice. "Let me tell it," she ordered. She cleared her throat.

Jessie sipped her hot chocolate. It was delicious! She took another sip.

"The hedge that protects the Realm," Maybelle began slowly and clearly, "is very powerful. The evil creatures in the Outlands have their own magic. But it isn't strong enough to destroy the hedge. Except once in a blue moon. Every fifty years, to be exact.

"The hedge, you see, is kept strong by magic. It's the same magic that keeps the whole of the

Realm running happily and smoothly. But every fifty years the magic runs out and has to be renewed. And this can only be done by the true Queen, using a spell that only she knows. If the magic isn't renewed, the hedge will crumble away." Maybelle paused. "Do you understand?" she asked abruptly.

Jessie nodded. "Of course I do!" she exclaimed. "And I suppose, from what the soldiers said, and because there's a blue moon in the sky, and because the hedge is dying, that the fifty years are nearly up now."

Giff groaned and buried his nose in his cup. "The mermaids are singing," he whimpered. "I don't know what they've got to sing about."

"The mermaids always gather in the Bay for the renewal," Patrice said, turning to Jessie. "They always sing. They're singing now because they believe, like everyone else, that everything is going to be all right."

"But you don't think so," said Jessie, looking at their worried faces.

Maybelle shook her head slowly. "Today at

dawn it'll be fifty years exactly since the magic was last renewed. Only a few grains are left. There should be enough to last till daybreak. But even now . . ."

"Oh!" cried Patrice, tearing off her apron and banging down her cup. "Oh, I can't stand it! I have to go and see."

"Me too, me too!" wailed Giff.

Maybelle snorted. "We'll all go," she said. "May as well know the worst." She jerked her head at Jessie. "You come with us," she said. "We can't leave you here alone. Someone might come in."

Jessie quickly finished her hot chocolate and then Patrice led the way from the kitchen, through her living room and out into a narrow corridor. The corridor led to some steep stairs, and then to yet another passageway that twisted and turned. The ceiling was very low. Jessie had to bend her head to follow the fat little woman toiling on ahead of her. Behind she could hear Giff panting and snuffling, and the neat clattering of Maybelle's hoofs on the floor.

They seemed to have been walking for a very

long time when finally Patrice stopped. In front of them was what looked like a wooden wall. There was a narrow gap in the wall, from where a board was missing, and through it soft light streamed. Patrice turned and put her finger to her lips, then faced the front again and crept forward, very slowly. She knelt and looked through the hole. The others quickly joined her.

The other side of the wall was covered by a gauzy curtain, but Jessie could see easily through the fine material. She found that she was staring straight into a huge, magnificently decorated room lit with hundreds of candles. Crystal pillars rose, glittering, to the high ceiling. Great windows lined one wall. Jessie realized that these were the windows she had seen when she was looking at the front of the palace. In the middle of the room a beautiful, gentle-looking woman sat on a golden throne. Red hair streamed over her shoulders and down her back, and on her head she wore a silver crown. She seemed to be deep in thought.

Beside the throne a huge, strangely shaped crystal jar, open at the top and the bottom, hung suspended in the air, shining in the candlelight. It was empty except for a few flecks of gold drifting slowly around at the very top. As they watched, one golden fleck began to fall downwards. After a minute or two it slipped from the bottom of the jar, hung in the air for a brief moment, and then disappeared with a tiny flash. The woman on the throne sighed and looked even more worried than before.

The four friends pulled themselves away from the wall and crept a little way back down the corridor so they could talk. Patrice clasped her hands. Her eyes were bright with fear.

"Listen," Jessie began. "Why doesn't the Queen just fix the magic now? She's sitting right beside it. She could just say the spell and . . ."

The other three shook their heads sadly. "Poor Queen Helena can't do anything about it," Patrice told her. "She's not the true Queen. She's a dear, sweet lady, and she's ruled us well and wisely, hasn't she, Giff?"

Giff nodded violently. "A bit soft-hearted, maybe," he said.

Patrice shrugged. "A bit too easily taken in by rogues and scoundrels, that's true. But that hasn't mattered up to now."

"Maybe not," Maybelle rumbled. "But in any case she's not the true Queen. She can't do a thing about the magic. She can't help at all."

"Well, where *is* the true Queen, then?" demanded Jessie. "Where is she? Why isn't she here?"

the sisters

"I'll tell you the story," said Maybelle. "Sit down."
Obediently, Jessie slid to the floor of the passageway and leaned against the wall. Giff and Patrice sat down beside her.

"Long ago," Maybelle began, "there were two little princesses in the Realm. One, the elder, would be Queen one day. It was she who learned from her mother the spell that would renew the magic. When the time came, only she would be able to make it work.

"She was beautiful, and willful, and charming, and everyone loved her. Her younger sister,

Helena, was also beautiful and beloved. But she was altogether softer tempered and gentler. A good, obedient child.

"The little princesses grew up together in the palace with their cousin Valda, who was about the same age and looked very like them both. Valda always acted sweet and well-behaved, but she had a cruel streak." Maybelle wrinkled her nose. "Valda was the sort of child who smiled at adults, but pinched and bullied smaller children when the adults weren't looking. You know what I mean."

Jessie nodded. She'd met one or two children like that.

Maybelle went on. "Despite their differences, the three girls played together, did their lessons together, and were like sisters. But all of them knew that Jessica would be Queen one day."

Jessie jumped. "What was that name?" she exclaimed.

Maybelle looked at her in surprise. "Jessica," she repeated. "Our true Queen. The one we were calling when we got you by mistake. Anyway . . . when Jessica was sixteen, a stranger visited the

Realm. He was tall and handsome—and from your world. He had found a Door, the same one you came through. There are many, if you know where to look."

"He loved it here," Giff put in, smiling sadly at the memory.

"So he did," Maybelle said, nodding. "He couldn't stay, because mortals can't survive in the Realm for long. But he visited us many times, over several years. He became friendly with many of the Folk. And every time he came, he went looking for Jessica."

"Everyone could see that they were falling in love," said Patrice, biting her lip. "But no one thought there was any harm in it. No one saw the danger at first. And then—"

"They ran away together," Jessie said slowly. "He took her back to his own world and they got married. His name was Robert Belairs."

They stared at her in surprise. "How do you know that?" asked Giff fearfully.

"Please go on," Jessie said to Maybelle. "Tell me all of it."

"They left on Jessica's twentieth birthday. The day that the magic was renewed by her mother, the Queen, and the blue moon hung in the sky," said Maybelle, still looking at Jessie curiously. "Jessica left a letter for her sister Helena. She said that when the time came, Helena should rule the Realm in her place. She said that though she must now live in the new world she had chosen, she would not forget us."

"She didn't take any of her beautiful clothes, or jewels, or anything," sighed Patrice, wiping her eyes. "She only took the charm bracelet that was hung with all her memories of home. In her letter to Helena she said she'd wear it always. It would stop her memory of the Realm from fading. It would help her to remember that in fifty years from that day she must come back — to renew the magic, anoint Helena's daughter as the next Queen, and keep the Realm safe."

"Oh, there was terrible trouble when the King and Queen found out what had happened," breathed Giff, his eyes wide.

"As you can imagine," said Maybelle dryly. "But

eventually they calmed down and saw that what was done, was done. They issued a proclamation saying that when the time came, Helena should take the throne, as Jessica had asked. And that Helena's child would be Queen after her. Almost everyone thought they were right. The people loved Jessica and were sad that she was gone. But they loved Helena, too."

"Valda wasn't happy, though," interrupted Giff, shivering.

"No." Patrice folded her arms and looked grim. "Valda wasn't happy at all. Valda was very angry. She claimed that Jessica had disgraced the royal family by what she'd done. She said that as Helena was Jessica's sister, she was disgraced, too. And she said that Helena was weak and would bring the Realm to ruin." She frowned. "Ah, she was a nasty, jealous, spiteful piece, that Valda, even as a girl."

"In a word," Maybelle said impatiently, "Valda said that she, Valda, should be anointed Queen in Helena's place. She gathered together some power-hungry, flattering creatures to support her. But she'd shown her true colors too soon. No one really wanted her as Queen."

"Eventually, the King and Queen, and the people, too, lost patience with her. They warned her many times, but she wouldn't stop her troublemaking. Finally, a plot to take Helena's life was discovered. And that was the end. The Queen banished Valda to the Outlands. And she hasn't been heard of since."

Patrice sighed. "So now, instead of three princesses, there was only one. Poor Helena. She was so lonely and afraid. She missed Jessica dreadfully. I remember it well. But in time she fell in love and was married, and took the throne. She had a child, a sweet girl, named Christie. And Helena has been a good Queen to us. A good and happy Queen. Now, though, she is in terrible trouble."

"Jessica said she'd come back," said Maybelle. "But she hasn't. And now evil stalks the Realm. The Doors to your world have been locked. But Helena didn't lock them. Someone else did."

"We three had to steal some of the last magic to force open the Door you came through," whispered Patrice to Jessie, clasping and unclasping her hands. "We were trying to call Jessica one last time. But she didn't come. I think . . . I think she must be dead." Tears welled up in her eyes.

"No!" Jessie grabbed her arm. "No, she isn't dead. She's at home. Jessica's my grandmother. The bracelet really must hold her memories of this place. Because she's lost it. And now she's forgotten what she has to do." She spun around to face Maybelle. "Quickly!" she rushed on. "Get me home! I'll bring Jessica back to you."

Maybelle shook her head. "It's too late," she said. "You can't do anything now. And besides —"

"Jessica!" The cry from the throne room was startling in the silence. Then there were sharp, ringing footsteps on the marble floor, and a tinkling sound that Jessie recognized.

The friends scuttled back along the passage to the curtained wall and peeped into the room beyond. Queen Helena had jumped to her feet and was facing someone they couldn't see. "Oh, Jessica," she was crying. "The magic is ebbing so fast, so fast! It is past midnight. The hedge is dying every moment you delay. And my guards say thousands of trolls are massing on the other side. Our people are becoming afraid. Please, please renew the magic now."

"Oh, the morning will be time enough, dear Helena," yawned another voice. "We have until dawn, after all. Just now I am tired to death. A relaxing bath and a soft bed are all I am planning on for the next few hours." There was a low laugh, and then a woman walked into view.

Jessie gasped.

The woman was small, and beautiful like Helena, with long, golden-red hair. She looked very like one of the great ladies in Robert Belairs' paintings. But her eyes were as cold as green ice, and her mouth was thin and proud. On her shoulder perched a pretty gray kitten that Jessie had seen before. And on her wrist was a bracelet. A charm bracelet, which tinkled as she looked around her, smiling at the room as though she owned it.

"Granny's bracelet!" breathed Jessie. "That woman's got Granny's bracelet!" She made a move to spring through the curtain, but Giff gasped in horror and Patrice grabbed her arm and held her back.

"Be still! Be quiet! She mustn't know you're here!" she hissed, pulling Jessie away from the curtain. "Or you'll disappear, as other people have." She tugged until Jessie moved with her and the others further down the passageway.

When they were far enough away not to be overheard, Jessie twisted around to face them. "Why does Queen Helena call that woman Jessica?" she demanded.

Maybelle curled her lip. "Because that woman says she's Jessica," she snorted. "And Helena believes her, as do most others here. Because she looks like Jessica. Because she came into the Realm at the right time. And because she's wearing Jessica's bracelet. To most people, the bracelet is proof of her identity."

"She stole the bracelet," exclaimed Jessie. "Or rather, her horrible cat stole it for her. He tripped Granny up and made her hurt her wrist so the bracelet had to be taken off. Then he took it and hid it, and waited till he got the chance to move it out of the house. I realize now. I actually saw him carrying it to the secret garden late last night. He was taking it back through the Door, to that woman, so she could pretend to be Granny." She turned to Maybelle. "But who is she?" she urged. "Why is she doing this?"

"We believe she's Valda," said Maybelle. Giff and Patrice nodded solemnly.

"We believe that for all these years of her exile she's been building her power, making her own evil magic, and planning her revenge," the little horse went on. "And now, when the Realm is at its weakest, she's returned to carry out her plan. She stole Jessica's bracelet to take away her Realm memories. And she used her own magic to lock the Doors, in case we tried to bring Jessica back ourselves. Jessica could undo her lock-spell in a moment. But we can't. Not without magic."

She sighed. "But why Valda's pretending to be Jessica, and why she claims she's going to renew the magic, when she knows she can't do it, we don't know. After all, she can't pretend she's Jessica forever. She *can't* renew the magic. In the end, everyone will find out that she's an imposter."

"The trouble is, by then the magic will be gone," muttered Patrice.

"Send me back!" cried Jessie. "Send me back quickly, and I'll bring the real Jessica to you. I will!"

They all looked at her sadly. "We can't," said Maybelle simply. "The Door is locked, and we don't have the magic to open it any more. We're very sorry. But we can't send you back. Ever."

jessie's plan

Later, Jessie couldn't remember how she'd got back to Patrice's cozy little kitchen. All she remembered was finding herself sitting at the table and crying, while Giff forlornly patted her arm and Patrice fussed around offering her cakes and drinks she couldn't swallow.

Maybelle stood shaking her head. "Sorry," she kept saying. "Very sorry."

"Sorry!" choked Jessie at last. She gave a shuddering sob. "What good's that? I want to go home!" She wiped her eyes with the back of her hand. Giff tremblingly offered her a green-and-white spotted handkerchief, and she took it. "I want to go home," she repeated more firmly.

Patrice clasped her little brown hands. "Oh, we wish we could help," she cried. "We'd do anything to help if we could."

"If only the real Jessica was here," moaned Giff, his drooping ears quivering. "Jessica would know what to do. Jessica would do something. Oh dear, oh dear!"

Jessie looked up. A memory stirred in her mind. She remembered her grandmother's laughing face and her voice: *Don't worry so. All will be well.* They were right. Granny wouldn't have given up. She lifted her chin.

"Well, *I'm* here," she said. "And I'm Jessica's granddaughter." Then she thought of something else. Some other words, spoken in her mother's calm, practical voice: *What we need round here is some common sense.* She raised her head higher. "I'm Jessica's granddaughter," she said, "and I'm Rosemary's daughter, too. And I'm not going to let any nasty old witch take over this place. Or steal my Granny's memory. *Or* stop me from getting home. I'm going to *make* her open the Door for me. And that's that!"

Giff stared at her admiringly.

"Oh, that's the way!" shrilled Patrice. "Oh, she does remind me of Jessica, Maybelle."

"That's as may be," retorted Maybelle. "But it's not as easy as all that. What exactly are you going to do, child, may I ask?"

The others waited expectantly.

"Well . . ." Jessie hesitated. Of course she hadn't the faintest idea. She shivered.

"You're cold!" exclaimed Patrice instantly. "Oh dear. I'll light a fire. And in the meantime . . ." She looked around and spied the old gray cloak lying on a chair by the door. She picked it up and handed it to Jessie. "Here," she said. "Put this on, dearie."

Thankfully, Jessie wrapped the cloak around her. Again she breathed in its warm, homey smell.

And then Giff screamed.

Jessie stared at him in surprise. The little elf was as pale as chalk. He was pointing at her with a shaking finger.

"What's the matter?" she asked.

"It's the cloak," exclaimed Patrice goggle-eyed. "That's what it is! Giff, stop that noise, for goodness sake! You're making my head spin!"

Maybelle moved away from her place in the corner and approached Jessie cautiously. She lifted her lips, felt carefully around, and then pulled at the cloak with her teeth until it fell away from Jessie's shoulders.

Patrice clapped her hands. "Told you!" she shrieked delightedly.

"Did you get this from your grandmother, child?" asked Maybelle, dropping the cloak to the ground.

"My name's Jessie!" Jessie snapped, feeling very ruffled. "And yes, it belongs to Granny. But why did you pull it off?"

"Because it makes you invisible, dearie," giggled Patrice. "You gave us such a fright. Didn't you know?"

Jessie stared. "No," she said blankly. "Invisible? But that's not true, Patrice. I wear it all the time at Blue Moon—I mean, at Granny's place. And there's no way it makes me invisible there."

"Well, it does here," said Maybelle with excitement. She pushed at the cloak with her nose. "My word, a cloak of invisibility! I haven't seen one of these for years."

"Only the royal family have them, Maybelle," said Patrice primly. She gathered the cloak up in her arms and smoothed its folds before handing it back to Jessie with a look of respect in her eyes.

Jessie stared at the soft gray material. Invisible! The word rang in her head. "Do you know where in the palace Valda is staying?" she asked suddenly.

Patrice nodded. "Of course. In Jessica's old bedroom," she said.

"Take me there, then," urged Jessie. "Come on! I've got a plan. I'll explain it to you as we go."

A guard stood outside the bedroom door. The four friends peeped at him cautiously from their hiding place behind a golden statue that stood in a turning of the passageway.

"What if she's already had her bath?" whispered

Patrice. "It's late. She might already be in bed."

"Then we'll have to play it by ear," Jessie whispered back. "Don't worry!" She pulled Granny's cloak around her shoulders and watched as the others blinked. She really was invisible! "Are you sure you want to go through with this?" she asked. "It'll mean trouble for you—afterwards."

"Of course we're sure," Patrice said, nodding. "Let's go."

"Good luck!" added Maybelle.

Giff waggled his ears and patted the air where he thought Jessie might have been.

With a wave that of course Giff and Maybelle couldn't see, Jessie slipped from behind the statue and, with Patrice beside her, walked up the corridor toward the guard. Patrice's shoes clattered on the polished marble floor. Jessie's bare feet made no sound at all. The guard stood staring straight ahead, unblinking and at attention, as they reached his side.

"The Lady will be wanting these," Patrice said to the guard. She showed him the two fluffy white towels she carried in her arms. He nodded and knocked at the door.

"Yes?" called a proud voice.

The guard winked at Patrice and opened the door. Patrice bustled into the room beyond, the invisible Jessie close behind her.

The walls of the bedroom were hung with pale blue curtains that fell to the floor in silky folds. The carpet was white and deliciously soft under Jessie's bare toes. The bedhead was painted with tiny blue and gold flowers to match the bed's silken spread. Through an open door a white marble bathroom could be seen. Jessie looked around her in wonder. It was hard to believe that this was where her grandmother had slept when she was a girl. It really was a room fit for a princess.

The woman they had seen in the throne room was standing in front of a tall mirror in the center of the room. Her red hair hung like a gleaming shawl down her back, and she was wearing a deep purple robe. The gray kitten sat at her feet.

"I brought you some fresh towels, my lady," said Patrice, dropping a deep curtsy.

"I already have towels, Patrice," said the woman coldly. "I had to ask for them earlier. Some silly girl brought them to me. It seemed you couldn't be found."

Patrice bowed her head. "It is my rest day today, my lady," she said.

"Rest day?" The woman's lips curved in a thin smile. "It seems you have all been spoiled while I have been away." She raised her hands to her hair and the charm bracelet on her wrist tinkled. "Helena is a dear girl, but far too soft. We shall see about all that—later."

"Yes, my lady," murmured Patrice, and bobbed another curtsy.

The woman's smile faded. She turned to face Patrice. "Don't think you can fool me with your curtsies and your 'my ladys,' Patrice," she sneered. "I know that you have been trying to cause trouble. You and that creature Maybelle, and the absurd Giff. I have . . . friends . . . who tell me what is going on in the palace."

"Spies, you mean," flashed Patrice, gripping the towels in her arms while her face blushed red.

"Friends," snapped the woman. "Loyal subjects who are pleased to have their true Queen home again."

"You aren't our true Queen," Patrice burst out. "You might fool everyone else, but you don't fool me. You aren't Jessica!"

In the corner Jessie put her hand over her mouth. Oh, not now! Oh, be careful, Patrice, she begged silently.

But the woman in front of the mirror only threw back her head and laughed. "You poor, silly creature. Who am I then?"

"You're Valda," cried Patrice. "I didn't nurse you, Jessica and Helena as babies for nothing. I'd know each one of you if I hadn't seen you for a hundred years. You were mean, spiteful and jealous as a child, Valda, and so you are now." The little servant was shaking with fear, but she stood up proudly.

Valda narrowed her eyes. "You never liked me, Patrice," she spat. "Never! And I didn't like you." She took a step forward, her fist raised. "You say one word to anyone about this and you'll regret it.

You'll regret it till the end of your days. Now get out! *Get out!*"

Patrice scuttled to the door, the towels still clutched in her arms. As she left the room she glanced back once, her small black eyes despairing.

Don't worry, Patrice, thought Jessie grimly. We're going to defeat her. And it's now or never.

the thief

W hen the door closed again and Valda believed herself to be alone, she turned back to the mirror and touched a finger to her smooth cheek. The gray kitten twined itself about her feet. She smiled.

"When morning comes, my little friend," she murmured to it, "these fools will pay for their treatment of me, for I will be Queen indeed. Jessica lies helpless in the mortal world, with no memory of the Realm. She will not stir to save her people now. The removal of the bracelet has seen to that. A few more hours and the last magic will have gone. The hedge will crumble. And my army from the Outlands will come in. Then the people of the Realm will see what it is to be ruled. They will learn to do exactly what they're told. Or face the consequences."

She smiled again, then turned and went toward the bathroom. Jessie held her breath, her ears straining. She heard the sounds of water running in the marble tub and Valda moving around. She heard the rustle of satin as the purple robe was tossed carelessly to the floor, and the clatter of slippers kicked aside. And then she heard the sound she had been waiting for. The tiny jingling of the charm bracelet as Valda removed it and put it down on the side of the bath before getting into the water. Jessie's heart leaped. She'd been certain that the bath would be the one place where Valda could not keep the bracelet on her wrist. And she'd been right.

Jessie stole to the bathroom door. Valda was lying in a billowing mass of scented, pale blue bubbles. Her hair was wound up in a white towel, her eyes were closed. The charm bracelet lay close beside her shoulder. Jessie held her breath and moved into the room. The white floor was cold and smooth under her feet. She made no sound.

Valda lay still. Jessie stretched out her hand for the bracelet. She took it between two fingers, and began to ease it toward her. And then she snatched it, jingling, from the edge of the bath, and ran for the door.

Valda's eyes flew open. She screamed with rage and grasped the slippery sides of the bath, struggling to get up.

"You're too late!" cried Jessie. "I've got Jessica's bracelet. I'm going to take it back to her, so her memory of the Realm will come back. And you can't stop me!" She threw open the bedroom door and darted out into the hallway. The guard on duty, flabbergasted, looked wildly right and left. He could hear Valda's shrieks of rage. He could hear Jessie's thudding footfalls and the tinkling of the bracelet. But he could see nothing at all.

Jessie pounded on, following the way Patrice had shown her. Sleepy guards and servants spun around gasping as they felt and heard her pass, then jumped as they became aware of Valda's furious shouting in the distance: "Stop her! Stop her!"

Panting, Jessie raced down the wide stairs that led to the ground floor and the main entrance. She could hear heavy feet coming after her now. The great golden doors were standing open. She began to run for them.

"Bar the doors! Quickly! Quickly!" shrilled Valda from the head of the stairs. Jessie glanced behind and saw her stamping in fury, wrapped in her purple robe, her red hair streaming. Dozens of soldiers and servants were thundering around her and down the stairs, running to catch the invisible thief. The guards at the entrance jumped to attention and started to swing the heavy doors shut.

But Jessie was too fast for them. She darted forward and just managed to dash between the doors as they closed. She glimpsed the startled eyes of one guard as he heard her pass. Then she was out in the open air and the doors were crashing shut behind her, and Valda was screaming in rage, "You fools! You fools!"

❅ ❅ ❅

Five minutes later, outside the Door where they had first met Jessie, Maybelle raised her head. She heard shouting and the sounds of many running feet, mingled with the distant music of mermaids' song. "Here we go," she said to herself. She lowered her head and began quietly nibbling the grass.

In moments the darkened roadway was alive with lights and people. Valda, black cloak flying, swept along at the head of the Royal Guard, the gray kitten perched on her shoulder. When she saw Maybelle she gasped, then frowned in deadly anger.

"You!" she breathed. "I might have known you'd be mixed up in this." She pointed a trembling finger at Maybelle. "All right! Where is the thief hiding?"

Maybelle raised her head and carefully licked up a piece of grass that was stuck to her bottom lip. "I beg your pardon?" she mumbled, her mouth full.

"Tell me!" Valda ordered. "Or it will be the worse for you!"

Maybelle twitched her ears. "I heard a jingling sound running past me and off up the road a few minutes ago," she said, turning her head to look to the left. "Someone was in an awful hurry. Running so fast I couldn't even see who it was."

"You're lying!" Spitting with rage, Valda whirled around to face the gaping soldiers. "Search!" she commanded. "The thief must be around here somewhere!"

"You're wasting your time," said Maybelle calmly. She crossed her front hoofs and watched with interest as the guards began stamping around the area.

Suddenly there was a pounce, a squeak and a cry of triumph. The guard Loris ran up to Valda, carrying a small, struggling figure under his arm.

"Ah . . ." hissed Valda. "Giff the elf. Giff the coward. And what are you doing out here so late, may I ask?"

"He was hiding in a tree, my lady," growled Loris, holding Giff out to show her. Giff trembled and chattered with fright.

"Tell me, Giff," cooed Valda, her eyes as cold as

green glass, "do you know anything about a thief?"

Giff jumped and squirmed in Loris's hand. His terrified eyes were fixed on Valda's.

"Speak!" snarled Valda. "And speak now. And then I may, I just may, spare your miserable life! If not . . ."

"No!" squeaked Giff. "No, don't hurt me, please. I'll tell! I'll tell!"

Maybelle snorted warningly.

"Ignore the horse," sneered Valda, still holding Giff's gaze. "She can't help you. No one can help you. You know where the thief is, don't you, elf? And you're going to tell me. Otherwise . . . !"

Giff covered his eyes with his hands and burst into tears. "She went through the Door!" he sobbed. "She had magic. She went through the Door!"

"What?" Valda wheeled around to face the hedge, her face a mask of baffled rage.

"Magic? But how . . . ?" She glared at Maybelle. "You thought you'd gain extra time for your sneaking thief by sending us off on a wild goose chase, didn't you?" she shouted. "You lying creature! You . . . !"

She pointed at the hedge. "Open!" she screamed. There was a sighing sound and a gust of cold air. And then, in the center of the hedge, an arched door appeared, shimmering and black.

"Go," said Valda to the kitten on her shoulder. "Bring the bracelet back to me. Do not fail!"

The creature sprang, hissing, from her shoulder and ran for the Door. It leaped into the blackness with a yowl.

Valda turned back to Maybelle. "So your plan to deceive me failed," she snarled. "Guards! Tether this horse and take it back to the palace. In the morning we will decide what its fate will be. The elf, too. Put it in chains!"

The guards looked at one another. Some of them weren't sure they liked this so-called Queen. They didn't like her frowns, or her cruelty, or her shouted orders. They didn't understand what was going on.

"Obey!" shrilled Valda. She watched as the guards slowly and sullenly did as she asked. She knew they were unhappy. But that didn't matter to her. In the morning she would have a proper troop of soldiers: the trolls and ogres who had sworn to obey her in return for gaining entrance to the Realm.

She frowned slightly at the thought of the stolen bracelet. How had the thief obtained a cloak of invisibility? How had the thief managed to open the Door? "Jessica!" Valda said to herself, and her frown deepened. She had thought that she had taken care of Jessica.

Then she raised her head. There was no need to worry. Soon it would be dawn. Then the Realm would be lost to Jessica and her kind forever. Valda smiled. She was too strong and too clever to be defeated now. Look how she had forced that stupid elf to tell her where the thief had gone.

Maybelle, tethered tightly and being led away between two guards, saw the smile. And despite her own trouble, and the pain of the ropes on her neck, she allowed herself a small smile, too.

She remembered Jessie's words as they had hurried through the palace hallways. "Once I've got the bracelet, we'll have to make Valda open the

Door so I can get back to Granny," she had said. "And the only way she'll do that is if she thinks I've gone through first."

"How do we make her think that?" Maybelle had asked. "She'll never believe us if we tell her."

Jessie had laughed. "No," she'd said. "But if she thinks she's *forced* someone to tell her, she'll believe, won't she?"

And then she'd turned to Giff and told him what she wanted him to do.

How angry Valda would be if she knew how she had been tricked. How angry if she had heard, as Maybelle had, the tiny tinkle of the charm bracelet as Jessie followed Valda's gray kitten through the Door that Valda herself had opened.

Maybelle plodded on. Good luck, Jessie, she thought. Good luck—and please hurry!

panic!

J essie ran from the secret garden, the bracelet clutched in her hand. The night was dark and cool, but she didn't think of that. All she thought of was reaching the house, of waking her grandmother, of giving her back the bracelet so her memory would return. Then Granny could get back to the Realm in time to renew the magic.

She saw that the back door of Blue Moon was still open, and saw the shadow of Flynn standing guard. She was nearly there —

And then, like a gray streak, Valda's creature was flying from the trees, tangling in her legs, and

Jessie was falling heavily onto the grass, her cloak twisting around her. And the creature was tearing at her hand with its claws, hissing and spitting, trying to make her give up the bracelet. It wasn't pretending to be a cute and helpless kitten now. It was showing its terrible strength.

"No!" shrieked Jessie desperately. "No!"

Flynn's growl was like rumbling thunder as he sprang. In a single bound he leaped from the doorstep to where Jessie had fallen. And then he was snarling at Valda's creature and beating it back, driving it away into the trees.

Jessie stumbled to her feet. Her wrist and the back of her hand were torn and bleeding, but she still had the bracelet. Behind her she could hear the two animals hissing and fighting. She didn't look back: she knew that Flynn could take care of himself. Her job was to give the bracelet to her grandmother.

The house was very still. Jessie crept to Granny's room and pushed the door open.

"Who is it?" asked a trembling voice. Granny was awake!

Jessie switched on the light. Her grandmother lay in bed, looking very small and pale, her white hair streaming over her shoulders and onto the covers.

"It's only me," whispered Jessie. She ran over to the bed and held out the charm bracelet. "Granny, I've found your bracelet."

"I couldn't sleep," mumbled the old lady. "There's something . . . I know there's something I've forgotten. Very important. So important. But I can't think what it is." She tossed her head on the pillows.

Jessie took Granny's unbandaged wrist gently in her hands. She fastened the bracelet around it with shaking fingers, then stood back.

Her grandmother looked at her for a long moment, and then in her eyes Jessie saw a spark, a light that grew and grew in strength. Granny gasped and struggled up on her pillows. "The Realm!" she panted. "My birthday!" She clasped Jessie's arm. "I . . . I have to get back to the Realm! Jessie . . . I have to renew the magic."

"I know," whispered Jessie. She tugged at her

grandmother's arm. "Granny, come with me now. We haven't much time. Valda is in the Realm, and everyone thinks she's you! She's planning to let the hedge die. And Maybelle, Patrice and Giff are in such trouble! You can save them! Oh, please come now. To the Door in the secret garden!"

Her grandmother threw aside the covers and tried desperately to push herself from the bed. But she was so weak! Jessie's heart sank. How would she ever walk all the way down to the secret garden?

Through the window she could see the sky was growing paler. It was nearly dawn!

"We have to hurry!" she said urgently. She put her arms around Granny's shoulders and tried to help her. But when the old woman was finally standing on the floor, Jessie realized it was hopeless. Her grandmother had been in bed too long, and was too frail to make the walk. Gently she pushed her back onto the bed.

"We have to find another way," she said.

Granny looked at her in despair. "I must find a Door," she breathed. "Another Door." She lifted her hand to her forehead and the bracelet jingled on her wrist. "I'm still . . . I can't quite remember everything," she said. "But I'm sure . . . I'm sure there was another way. I'm sure Robert said . . ."

Jessie's heart leaped. "Yes!" she exclaimed. "Wait, Granny. I know. I know!"

She left her grandmother sitting staring after her and rushed from the room, the gray cloak flying behind her. Quietly, quietly, she told herself. If Mum wakes up we'll never be able to explain in time.

She ran on tiptoe to the studio. The painting was standing where she had last seen it. As she picked it up she saw again the card on the back. *For my princess on her birthday. Better to be safe than sorry. All my love, always, Robert.*

Good, careful, practical Robert Belairs. The man who had fallen in love with a fairy princess, but always kept his feet on the ground. Robert had always believed in preparing for the worst. Before he died, he had made for his princess a painting that was a spare key to her old home.

Jessie staggered through the shadowy corridors

of Blue Moon, the painting clutched firmly in her arms. It was heavy, and her injured hand hurt. But she didn't stop until she'd reached her grandmother's room again and had put the painting on the floor.

As her grandmother stared at it, another veil of confusion and forgetfulness lifted from her eyes. She smiled. "Robert!" she breathed, her voice full of love. She reached for Jessie's hand. "I must go," she said.

"Take me with you," urged Jessie. "You need help. I'll help you."

Granny squeezed her fingers. "Leave on the cloak, then," she said. "So Valda will not see you. Are you ready?"

Jessie nodded. She saw her grandmother's green eyes flash. "Open!" said a voice she hardly recognized. And then Granny was gripping her hand even more tightly, and Jessie was shivering in a breath of cool wind. The archway in the painting seemed to grow larger and larger, until it was filling all her sight . . .

And then they were no longer in the bedroom

at Blue Moon. They were somewhere else. Not on the roadway beside the dying hedge, where the dawn was staining the sky golden pink and the blue moon was setting. Not in the forest, where the pale-leaved trees rustled their fear in the mauve light. Not in front of the golden palace, where a crowd of anxious people—fairies, elves, gnomes, pixies, creatures of every shape and sort—had gathered, waiting. But in the throne room, under the light of a thousand candles. Beside the twinkling crystal jar, where one last gold fleck drifted slowly downwards.

"What is the meaning of this?" thundered a voice.

Jessie spun around. In an instant her gaze took in the people around her. Queen Helena, looking terrified, stood with her daughter, Christie. A crowd of guards and finely dressed fairy folk, serious-faced dwarves, elves and pixies, huddled behind her. And in one corner of the room were the bowed figures of Patrice, Maybelle and Giff, wound round with chains.

But right in the center of the huge room stood

another figure. A figure wearing a dress of deepest blue and a crown of gold. Valda. Valda, frowning thunderously, pointing at the frail elderly woman standing motionless and apparently alone, her hand on the crystal jar.

"Who is this old crone who dares to break into my palace!" she shrieked. Her eyes widened. "She is wearing my bracelet!" she choked. "The thief!" She whirled around to face the guards. "Take her away!" she ordered.

The guards hesitated.

"What are you waiting for!" screamed Valda. "Are you afraid? Of a silly old woman? Of a nobody, alone and unprotected? Take her away! I command you!"

Two of the guards reluctantly stepped forward.

Jessie glanced at her grandmother in panic. Her head was bent. The hand that rested on the crystal jar was trembling. Granny needed time. Jessie untied the ribbons that held the cloak around her neck. The cloak dropped to the floor. The people gasped as she appeared before their eyes.

"She's not alone!" shouted Jessie. "And she isn't a nobody! She's . . ."

"Jessica!" The cry echoed through the room. And Patrice was staggering forward, pulling at the chains that bound her, her eyes streaming with tears. "Jessica!"

A great shout rose up from the crowd. The guards fell back. Helena stood as if frozen, her hands pressed to her mouth.

"Absurd!" shrilled Valda. "I am Jessica!" But her voice was full of dread as well as anger.

Jessie glanced fearfully at her grandmother. Granny's eyes were fixed on the last fleck of gold as it drifted slowly, slowly downwards. When it reached the bottom of the jar it would float out into the air and disappear. And then . . .

"Granny, the spell," Jessie urged her. "The words! Say the words!"

Her grandmother turned her head and looked at Jessie. "If only I had more time," she said, her voice very low. "More memories are coming back to me every second. But the words . . . Jessie, I can't remember the words!"

CHAPTER TEN

"Remember . . ."

"S he's a fraud!" screeched Valda, her eyes fixed greedily on the drifting gold speck. It had nearly reached the bottom of the jar now. "A thief and a fraud! And if you won't remove her from this chamber, I will!" She strode across the room toward Jessica, her hands, tipped with long, pointed nails, outstretched.

"No!" cried Helena. She sprang and caught Valda around the waist. Valda turned, hissing, and tried to push her away. "Jessica!" sobbed Helena. "Oh, my Queen, my sister! Help us!"

At the sound of her sister's voice, Granny's

green eyes flashed with memory. The bracelet tinkled on her wrist as she stretched out her hand again and began to move it over the crystal. Then softly, softly, she began to sing, a strange, lilting song with words that didn't rhyme: "Blue moon floating, mermaids singing, elves and pixies, tiny horses, dwarves and fairies . . ."

Jessie's heart lurched. She was the only one close enough to hear the words. And she knew them! These were the words she'd heard so often when Granny sang to her at night. For all these years, Granny had been singing the spell!

Granny took a deep breath and closed her eyes. She wasn't sure what came next! Jessie put her arm around her and leaned forward till her lips touched her grandmother's ear: "Wait together, in the silence," she breathed.

Granny's eyes opened again. And this time they were full of light. "Wait together, in the silence," she sang, "waiting for the magic rain. Come down, come down, come down and gather, I the Queen command it now!"

There was a moment's electric silence. Then,

without a sound, the last gold fleck drifted from the crystal jar. It hung in the air, winking, in its last instant of life.

Valda shrieked with triumph. Helena screamed and hugged Christie tight. The candles flickered and dimmed . . .

And then the room blazed. Blazed with golden light. And the crystal jar was twisting and turning in the air, filling to overflowing with millions upon millions of chips of solid sunshine that sprayed out and over the top and showered the amazed people with glittering glory. The gold shot up to the ceiling and beat against the windows like sparks from a thousand fireworks.

In the center of the shimmering, whirling mass of gold stood Jessica. But no longer was she frail and old. Now she was again the Jessica of the paintings—young, lovely and triumphant, holding up her arms, shaking back thick, long hair that was no longer white, but shining red.

Jessie blinked, laughed, stared in amazement, hugged herself with relief. With overwhelming happiness she heard a great roar rising up from the crowd outside the palace, as the people saw the dazzling light and broadly smiling guards swung open the windows to let their cheering in.

With a cry of rage, Valda made a dash for the door. But a row of guards stepped forward to block her way. She spun around and shouted to Jessica.

"Queen Jessica, I am your cousin! Do not harm me. Let me go!"

Jessica stepped forward. "You are my cousin, Valda," she said gravely. "But you are my enemy, too. My enemy, and the enemy of all the Realm." She sighed. "We will not harm you. That is your way, but not ours. We will simply again put you out of our sight." She lifted her hand. "By my power as Queen, in the time of renewal of the magic," she said, "I banish you once more to the Outlands. This time, the magic will hold. Now, go!" She pointed a stern finger. And with a final shriek, Valda dissolved before their eyes and disappeared into the air.

An hour later, Jessie and her grandmother stood by the hedge, which stretched high and glossy green before them. On one side of them stood Helena and her daughter Christie, and on the other stood Patrice, Maybelle and Giff.

"Oh, Jessica, why won't you stay!" begged Helena, with tears in her beautiful eyes. "This is your home! We need you!"

Jessica shook her head. "No," she smiled. "My home is in the world of mortals now. I made that choice long ago, Helena, and I don't regret it. It's brought me so much happiness." She laid her hand on Jessie's arm.

"And you don't need me, Helena," she went on, gently. "You'll go on ruling the Realm as well as ever. And only half an hour ago you saw me anoint Christie as the Queen to come after you. You know I've taught her the words to renew the magic when her turn comes." She smiled at the girl, who smiled shyly back. "So the burden has been lifted from my shoulders, and the future of the Realm is secure."

"You will come and visit, though, won't you?" pleaded Giff. "You or Jessie. Please?"

"Oh, please!" echoed Patrice.

"It might be just as well," Maybelle put in gruffly. She coughed. "For a human, the girl seems to be rather useful."

Jessica smiled again. "Ah well," she said. "We'll see. I feel it would be best for me to keep away. But Jessie's a different matter. And if she wants to, and you're willing . . ."

Helena stepped forward and pressed something into Jessie's hand. "You have done us a great service, Jessie," she said. "We give you this as a token of our love and thanks."

Jessie looked. In her hand was a chain bracelet. A single golden charm hung from it. A heart.

"Every time you visit us," said Helena, "another charm will be added. And this way you will always remember us. The Doors are all open again now, my dear. You will always be welcome. You have only to wish."

Jessica's green eyes warmed as she fastened the bracelet on her granddaughter's wrist. "Jessie will be back," she said. "Oh, yes."

The sisters and friends hugged and kissed each other. Giff was crying openly, and even Maybelle was seen to snort away a tear or two. Then Jessica turned towards the Door. "Open!" she said. The archway appeared, and with a rushing sound she and her grandmother moved through it to the other side.

Rosemary stepped through the doorway into the secret garden. She gasped. Her mother and her daughter were standing there in the center of the lawn, bathed in sunlight. She rubbed her dazzled eyes. For a moment, just for a moment, her mother's long, flowing hair had looked as bright and red as Jessie's. But when she looked again, of course, Jessica's hair was quite white. It must have been a trick of the sunlight, she thought.

"Mum! Jessie! I was so worried about you!" she exclaimed. "Neither of you were in your beds! What possessed you to come out so early? Jessie, Granny should be resting."

"Oh no, Rosemary darling," smiled Granny. "Today's my birthday! And I'm much better now. So much better."

They began walking back to the house. "Mum,

you're . . . you're walking so well! And you've found your bracelet," said Rosemary, noticing the bright gold on her mother's wrist.

"Jessie found it for me," laughed Granny. "And now she's got one of her own."

Rosemary looked at her shrewdly. "Something's happened, hasn't it, Mum?" she said. "You've got that look in your eye like you used to have when I was little."

The charm bracelet tinkled on Granny's wrist. She looked around and sighed contentedly, breathing in the sweet mountain air. "It's a beautiful, beautiful day," she said.

Rosemary stopped. "You're not going to move to town and live with us, Mum, are you?" she said suddenly.

"No, darling," Granny answered. "I'm better here. But I've been thinking. Instead of me coming to live with you, you and Jessie could . . ."

"Oh no!" laughed Rosemary, holding up her hand. "Oh no. We can't move! What about my job? And Jessie's school? What about . . .?"

"Nurse Allie said there were several jobs for

nurses at the hospital here," said Granny. "Good jobs."

"And there's a school here," Jessie put in eagerly. "A good school."

Rosemary regarded them both helplessly. "I'll think about it," she said at last.

Jessie and her grandmother exchanged happy looks. They both knew what her decision would be.

"This has been a wonderful birthday morning," said Granny. "I'll never forget it." She smiled and tapped her bracelet. "Now, I'll never forget it."

Jessie looked at her own bracelet, shining gold against her tanned wrist. "No," she said, thinking of all she'd done and seen, and of all the adventures still to come. "Neither will I."

Turn the page for a peek at
Jessie's next adventure in the

FairyRealm:
BOOK 2

the flower fairies

M aybelle pawed the grass with her front hoof. "I thought it was about time you came back to see us," she said. "The Realm's got shocking problems at the moment, and we could do with a hand."

"What shocking problems?" demanded Jessie. "Surely you've got all the magic you need now." She pointed. "More than enough, I'd say. You've got it all over your ribbons."

Maybelle snorted irritably and shook her mane so that flecks of gold flew into the air and whirled in the sunbeams. Jessie felt little thrills like tiny electric shocks as some of the shining specks fell on her skin. She shivered and giggled.

Maybelle glared at her. "Now don't you get silly too," she ordered. "I've got enough problems with that in the Realm. That's the trouble with magic. There always seems to be too much of it, or too little. When you came to the Realm last time, we were running out of it, and thanks to you that problem was solved. But now we've got too much.

And that's another problem altogether."

"Too much magic?" Jessie giggled again. She could still feel little thrills of excitement all over her arms and face. "How can there be too much magic?"

Maybelle sighed deeply. "They say it always happens just after the magic is renewed," she said. "There's an explosion of it, see, and then for ages afterwards the dust gets into everything. And everyone," she added darkly. "You should see Giff. That elf is just about uncontrollable. Silly as a wheel. And the flower fairies are worse than he is. They're not terribly sensible at the best of times, in my opinion. But now . . . hopeless!"

Jessie bit her lip to keep her giggles back, and nodded sympathetically.

"But the griffins are the real reason I've come to see you," Maybelle grumbled on. "They're the Queen's pets. And they're supposed to guard the Realm's treasures. Well, that's fine. Let them guard the treasures. No one's arguing about that. But they're not supposed to get so full of themselves that they take over guarding everything else too. Are they?"

4

"I suppose not," Jessie murmured.

"I'd give anything for a bit of peace and quiet," Maybelle complained. "I'd like just for once to wake up in the morning without my mane and tail all full of giggling fairies. Just for once to have a quiet bowl of oats for breakfast, or a bit of sugar maybe, without having to fight some griffin to get it." She looked up. "You wouldn't by any chance have some sugar about you at the moment, would you?" she asked hopefully.

"No, sorry," said Jessie. "But I could go up to the house and get you some, if you like. Or some bread. Everything's still on the table from breakfast."

Maybelle licked her lips. "Thanks," she said. "Thanks for the offer. But on the whole I'd rather you just came through to the Realm with me right now and tried to sort the griffins out. You're good with magic. That was obvious last time. So—"

"But I'm *not* good with magic," cried Jessie. "Granny's the one who knows about it. She's the one who renewed the Realm's magic. All I did was bring her to you. And to do that I just used human common sense."

"Well, whatever you used, it worked," Maybelle said, nodding. "And I'd be very grateful if you'd stop arguing with me, and come and do it again!" She pursed her lips and tapped the ground with her hoof, waiting.

Jessie grinned. She really didn't think she'd be able to help Maybelle with her problem. But of course she was dying to have an excuse to visit the Realm again. And it *was* Saturday. There was nothing else she had to do, except clean up after breakfast. Mum and Granny had gone shopping and wouldn't be back for an hour or two. So why not?